common threads

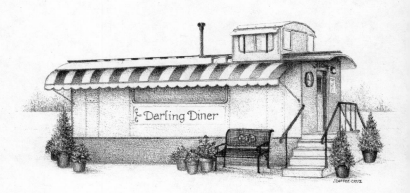

Darling Diner

common
threads

a novel

Patty Bultman

with Jennifer Jackson

Tate Publishing & Enterprises

Common Threads: The Peace House Series
Copyright © 2011 by Patty Bultman. All rights reserved.

Scriptures taken from the *Holy Bible, New International Version*®, NIV®. Copyright © 1973, 1978, 1984 by Biblica, Inc.™ Used by permission of Zondervan. All rights reserved worldwide. www.zondervan.com

This novel is a work of fiction. However, several names, descriptions, entities, and incidents included in the story are based on the lives of real people.

The opinions expressed by the author are not necessarily those of Tate Publishing, LLC.

Published by Tate Publishing & Enterprises, LLC
127 E. Trade Center Terrace | Mustang, Oklahoma 73064 USA
1.888.361.9473 | www.tatepublishing.com

Tate Publishing is committed to excellence in the publishing industry. The company reflects the philosophy established by the founders, based on Psalm 68:11,
"The Lord gave the word and great was the company of those who published it."

Book design copyright © 2011 by Tate Publishing, LLC. All rights reserved.
Cover design by Rebekah Garibay
Interior design by Chelsea Womble

Published in the United States of America

ISBN: 978-1-6177-263-4
Fiction, Christian
11.03.15

To my husband Alan, you are more than I could have ever asked for or imagined. You were truly picked by God, especially for me.

acknowledgements

Thanks to God for allowing me to be involved in His plan for this miracle. To Julie, Jan, Lizann, Patty, and Jennifer; thank you for helping to make this book a reality.

Thank you to Tate Publishing for believing in this project.

I am especially grateful for my family and friends. Thank you so much for your support.

Thank you readers, I pray you will find peace, hope and healing.

And I pray that you, being rooted and established in love, may have power, together with all the saints, to grasp how wide and long and high and deep is the love of Christ, and to know this love that surpasses knowledge—that you may be filled to the measure of all the fullness of God.

Ephesians 3:18–19 (NIV)

Prayer of St. Francis

Lord, make me an instrument of your peace;

where there is hatred, let me sow love;

where there is injury, pardon;

where there is doubt, faith;

where there is despair, hope;

where there is darkness, light;

where there is sadness, joy;

O divine Master,

Grant that I may not so much seek to be consoled
as to console;

to be understood, as to understand;

to be loved, as to love;

for it is in giving that we receive,

it is in pardoning that we are pardoned,

And it is in dying that we are born to Eternal life.

Amen

For God so loved the world that he gave his one and only Son, that whoever believes in him shall not perish but have eternal life.

John 3:16 (NIV)

chapter one

Abigail loved to spend time sanding and painting old furniture, transforming each piece into something beautiful. She could spend hours recovering an antique chair or distressing an old dresser. Most people wouldn't look twice at the items Abigail so tenderly made-over. To others they were junk, but to Abigail each project she worked on was a treasure. She saw the potential hidden beneath the shabby outward appearance.

Her love for transformation wasn't limited to furniture. More than anything, she loved seeing people transformed, especially when they experienced the love of Jesus. Her life's mission was to be His hands and feet. She wanted to witness changed lives, to see others touched and changed by the love of Jesus, the way she had been when she first experienced His love.

Abigail owned an interior design shop in a small town, deep in the heart of the Bible belt. It was your typical small town, full of gossip and politics. From the outside the people seemed friendly, but many times their smiles hid long-kept secrets, and they were quick to judge others.

She had learned quickly that within their small society lived many poor, lonely, and rejected people. Too often they found themselves shunned by the local churches and the overly religious, who were more concerned about following a set of religious rules than experiencing a loving relationship with Jesus Christ.

It wasn't long after Abigail had moved to the small Bible belt town that she had her first encounter with someone who didn't exactly share her joy for the Lord.

Abigail could vividly remember the first time she met Mimsey Magness. She had just begun to transform the old house she had bought into Abigail Kurtain Interiors. Abigail had been knee deep in boxes and bolts of fabric when Mimsey walked through the door. Mimsey was the local insurance agent, a very classy lady, always dressed in the most recent styles.

That day, Mimsey had been wearing a pair of flattering designer jeans and a cashmere sweater. Her flats and handbag had matched perfectly. Abigail had felt a little self-conscious in her jeans and t-shirt.

"Hi, my name is Mimsey," she said as she looked around at the mess that surrounded Abigail. "I'm the insurance agent in town." Abigail was embarrassed to meet Mimsey for the first time amidst the disaster.

"Hi, I'm Abigail Kurtain." Abigail wiped her dusty hands on her pant leg and extended her hand to Mimsey.

Mimsey shook her hand quickly but looked disapprovingly at Abigail's un-manicured hands. "Could you use a break?" she asked. "I could run across the street and get you something to drink."

"An iced tea would be lovely," Abigail said. "I've been working hard the past few days to get the store in order. I'm getting close to opening up for business."

"Two iced teas coming right up," Mimsey said as she headed towards the door. "Maybe we can enjoy that front porch swing when I get back."

"Sounds great," Abigail said. "I'll meet you on the porch in a few minutes."

After Mimsey left to get the drinks, Abigail took a few minutes to freshen up. She washed her hands, pulled her long blond hair into a ponytail and added a touch of gloss to her lips.

Feeling a little better about her appearance, Abigail went out to the porch to wait for Mimsey. A few minutes later Mimsey returned with the iced tea and the two women sat on the cozy porch swing chatting about small town life.

The swing was an antique. It was made of wicker, woven together very ornately. Abigail loved sitting on it, especially early in the mornings. She had draped a soft quilt across it, making it an ideal spot for good conversation.

Something about Mimsey intrigued Abigail and she wanted to find out more about the woman. Based on their small talk, she sensed Mimsey knew a lot about the town and its people; maybe even a little too much. She seemed nosey.

"So, how long have you lived here, Mimsey?" Abigail asked as she sipped her iced tea.

"Born and raised here," Mimsey said. "I went away to college but returned after I graduated and married my college sweetheart. It was the wedding of the year." She said as she smiled. "My husband started farming with my father, and we've been here ever since."

Abigail could tell Mimsey wasn't thrilled to be living in a small town. It seemed to Abigail that a fast-paced life in the city would better suit Mimsey, a life full of designer clothes and social events.

"Wow! Wedding of the Year," Abigail said teasingly. "I love weddings; you'll have to bring pictures by sometime and share all the details with me. I was a wedding planner and florist for twenty-five years and never get tired of romantic wedding stories.

"It must have been nice to have found Mr. Right while you were in college," Abigail continued. "When it came to men, I was told my picker was broke. I picked a few bad ones before I discovered that God had already hand-picked a husband just for me."

"Oh, I didn't need God to pick out my husband," Mimsey said. "One look at Jim and I knew I would marry him. I think I did ok. We have good jobs, a nice house, and a son in medical school."

"Well, it took me a while to find Mr. Right, but Adam is definitely God's plan for my life," Abigail said. "We've only been married a few months."

"Congratulations," Mimsey said. Abigail could tell Mimsey was feeling uncomfortable. The conversation seemed to be getting a little too heavy for her.

"I know you need to get back to work," Mimsey said. "I'll just spill the real reason for my visit. I was just wondering if you needed any insurance coverage on your new shop."

Abigail was surprised at the sudden change and mood in conversation. She had a sneaky suspicion that Mimsey was uncomfortable talking about God. She also sensed that she had some regrets about how her small town life had turned out.

"I will visit with Adam about the insurance tonight," Abigail said kindly. "He takes care of stuff like that. I prefer to stick to the creative stuff, like interior design."

"Well okay," Mimsey said as she stood up to leave. "I'll check back in a few days and see how things are coming with the store. I can't wait to see your selection. It'll be nice to have a specialty store here in town. When do you plan to open?"

"Monday," Abigail said. "Still have a lot to do over the next few days, but I'm making progress. I'd love for you to come by when the store opens and see all the great things I've ordered. After you shop, we can chat over tea and homemade muffins."

"That sounds delightful," Mimsey said.

Abigail stood up and went to give Mimsey a hug, but she quickly stuck out her hand. Abigail took it and gave it a squeeze. Mimsey was obviously not a hugger.

Abigail watched as Mimsey strolled down the sidewalk. After she had turned the corner, Abigail went back inside to try and organize the piles of merchandise she would sell in her shop.

--- --- --- --- --- --- --- --- --- --- --- --- --- ---

Abigail had dreamed of owning an interior design business and specialty shop for years. She had spent many hours tediously going over the plans to transform the old Victorian home into Abigail Kurtain Interiors.

Abigail prayed her shop would be a place where customers felt welcome and at peace. She wanted

17

them to pull up a chair, enjoy a cup of tea, and stay awhile.

Blooming azalea bushes lined the front of Abigail's shop and red geraniums graced the front steps. The smell of homemade muffins encouraged visitors to step inside and experience all that the shop had to offer.

Sunlight spilled through the windows bathing everything in a warm, golden hue. Gorgeous tapestry rugs adorned the antique hardwood floors and bolts of deep plum, emerald, and gold fabrics were displayed along the shop's back wall.

A beautiful black table, glazed with swirls of gold, cream, and chocolate brown, sat in the dining room. Abigail always had a variety of coffees, teas, and specialty chocolates for her guests to enjoy.

The room located to the north of the dining room was filled with antique books. A tall, rolling ladder made it easy for guests to search the literary treasures located on the top shelves. A library table sat in the center of the room adorned with a fragrant candle, an old quill pen, and pretty stationery. Abigail hoped the room would inspire some of her guests to sit down and write letters. She loved hand-written notes and letters. They were such a source of encouragement to the person who received them. There was always an ample supply of note cards and stamps ready for customers to use.

The furniture that Abigail sold resembled designer brands but didn't carry a designer price tag. Abigail had spent many hours refurbishing it. She took pride in the fact that no two pieces were the same. Each one was created as uniquely as God had created people.

In addition to Abigail being an excellent designer, with a keen eye for style, she had a knack for helping people find the perfect gift for their special occasion. Her gift wrapping was almost as special as the gift, and many times the recipient was hesitant to rip through the beautiful paper.

But more important than the material gifts she hoped to help her customers find was Abigail's desire to share the gift of Jesus with them.

She was a firm believer that God had a purpose and plan for His children. She knew that He had called her to encourage women and share His love with them, even if it was by selling them one gift at a time.

Do not store up for yourselves treasures on earth, where moth and rust destroy, and where thieves break in and steal. But store up for yourselves treasures in heaven, where moth and rust do not destroy, and where thieves do not break in and steal.

Matthew 6:19–20 (NIV)

chapter two

One morning, not long after Abigail's shop had opened for business, she heard rustling outside the back door. Abigail peeped out the window to see a woman, probably in her mid-fifties, rummaging through some of the boxes she had thrown out.

The woman was wearing a knee-length tweed coat, the color of ferns. The coat had two patch-work pockets, and big rhinestone buttons adorned the front. Abigail had never seen such a sight.

"Hi," Abigail said, "Do you need boxes? You're welcome to take any of those."

The sound of Abigail's voiced startled the lady in the green coat.

"I'm always looking for stuff," the lady said. "But not boxes in particular. But I might be able to use some of these for something."

Abigail walked down the back steps to introduce herself.

"My name is Abigail," she extended her hand. The lady took Abigail's hand and shook it gently, but wouldn't make eye contact with her.

"My name is Ruthie Jones, but Ruthie will work just fine," she said. "Call me Ruthie."

"Well why don't you call me Abi," Abigail smiled at her. "I love the name Ruthie. It reminds me of one of my favorite books of the Bible, the book of Ruth."

"I love that book as well," Ruthie said as she started to stack one box inside another. "I think that's where my mother got my name."

"Would you like to come inside for a cup of tea?" Abigail asked.

"No thanks, I better get going," Ruthie said, her arms full of boxes. Before Abigail could tell her goodbye, she was headed towards an old station wagon parked in the alley.

"Nice to meet you, Ruthie, please come back and visit will you?" Abigail said loudly.

Ruthie didn't turn around. She put the boxes into her station wagon and drove away.

- -

Abigail spent the next week watching Ruthie walk up and down the alley in her fern green coat. Her arms were usually full of items that she had discovered along her journey.

Abigail was intrigued by Ruthie. She couldn't understand why she spent her days rummaging through dumpsters and collecting items that people had left, never expecting anyone to ever use again. Abigail decided it really was true that one man's junk was another man's treasure.

One morning Abigail was sitting on the front porch swing when Ruthie walked by.

"Hi, Ruthie," Abigail said as she waved to her. "Can I talk to you for a minute?"

Ruthie walked up the porch steps slowly, not sure why Abigail would want to talk to her. It was obvious the two women had completely different lifestyles. Abigail owned a beautiful shop full of pricey furniture and gifts. Ruthie lived in a structure about the size of a garden shed, drove a faded station wagon that was more than twenty years old, and had few material possessions to her name. She wasn't sure what she and Abigail could possibly have in common.

Abigail loved to decorate houses, and that didn't interest Ruthie in the least bit. She thought it was a waste of time to store treasures on earth. She focused on storing her treasures in heaven.

"Would you like some tea?" Abigail asked.

Ruthie hesitated, not sure what to make of Abigail's kindness and hospitality. Most of the people in town stayed as far away from Ruthie as they could. She made them feel uncomfortable, and they weren't the kind of people who liked to be forced outside of their comfort zone.

"Yes, a cup of tea would be good. With two cubes of sugar, please," Ruthie said.

Abigail motioned for her to sit in a chair across from the porch swing. Ruthie sat down and placed the bags she had been carrying at her feet. Abigail handed her the steaming cup of tea and sat on the swing.

"Do you live close by?" Abigail asked as Ruthie carefully sipped the hot tea.

"I actually live in a small house behind your shop. Just across the alley," Ruthie said.

Abigail remembered seeing the house, but to her, it looked more like a shed. As Abigail watched

Ruthie drink her tea, she noticed a pin, in the shape of a cross that Ruthie wore. It was fastened to the lapel of her coat.

"Ruthie, that's a beautiful broach," Abigail said.

"Thank you," Ruthie said. "A friend gave it to me and I promised her I would never take it off. It reminds me always that Jesus is with me."

Abigail was so excited! For the first time since she had moved to the small town, she was having a conversation with someone who wasn't afraid to talk about Jesus outside of church.

Ruthie seemed just as willing as Abigail was to share her love for Jesus.

"Ruthie, I think you and I are going to be great friends," Abigail said.

Ruthie looked confused.

"What makes you think that? We are two completely different people. I have no interest in interior design or fancy things," Ruthie said.

"Our outside appearances may be different, but on the inside we are just the same," Abigail said. "We both love Jesus. That is a great reason to be friends."

Ruthie sat silent for a few minutes, taking in Abigail's excitement. It didn't take long before

Ruthie realized she liked Abigail. She had a lot of joy bottled up inside of her and seemed to genuinely care about people, even people she didn't know. Ruthie decided it probably wouldn't hurt to have a friend; she didn't have many around town anyways.

"Didn't you say I could call you Abi?" Ruthie asked.

Abigail nodded her head as Ruthie continued with her thoughts.

"I know you like to decorate things and make them nice," Ruthie said. "What if I brought you some old furniture and other items to redo? Maybe you could even sell them in your shop."

"Oh, Ruthie, that would be wonderful," Abigail said. "I would just love that."

"I've already got a few things you might like," Ruthie said. "I'll bring them to you."

Ruthie stood up and grabbed her bags and started to walk towards the steps. Abigail smiled as she watched her new friend walk down the street. Maybe Jesus wouldn't be the only thing that she and Ruthie bonded over.

- -

Over the next few months Ruthie and Abigail's friendship blossomed.

Ruthie would show up at Abigail's back door several times a week with a special treasure for her to restore. Abigail loved to see what her friend had found during her excursions through the alleys in town.

It was amazing what people were willing to leave in the dumpster. Several of the pieces were antiques and were probably worth something of value.

As Abigail and Ruthie spent more time together, Abigail realized that there was something very special about her friend. She didn't know very much about Ruthie's past or why she chose to live the way she did, but she knew she loved the Lord.

Ruthie glowed with the love of Jesus more than anyone Abigail had ever seen. Abigail believed God placed people in her life for a reason. She felt strongly that God had a bigger purpose for bringing Ruthie into her life; much bigger than worn-out furniture in need of restoring.

"For I know the plans I have for you,"
declares the Lord. "Plans to prosper you and
not to harm you, plans to give you hope and
a future."

Jeremiah 29:11 (NIV)

chapter three

A loud knock came from the back door, startling Abigail. It had to be Ruthie. Except for delivery people, she was the only one who used the back door of the shop.

"Hey, Ruthie, you startled me," Abigail said.

Ruthie was holding a box and had a concerned look on her face. Abigail could tell something was up.

"Ruthie, are you okay?" she asked. "You look upset."

"Abigail, look what I found."

Ruthie walked into the dining room and placed a sage green box, slightly bigger than a hat box, on the table.

"I found this among a pile of stuff sitting next to a dumpster," Ruthie said. She dusted off the lid, untied the ribbons, and lifted the lid of the box to reveal the contents inside. "It's not just a box full of books. It is filled with letters, very personal letters. I'm not sure who the owner is or why it was left by the dumpster, but I need to find a way to get this box back to the person it belongs to."

"My goodness, slow down. If the owner left the box in a pile of trash, they must not want it." Abigail said, trying to console her friend. She had to admit the box looked nothing like the items Ruthie usually found on her excursions through the alley.

"They have to want it! There are so many personal letters in here and I'm sure each one has a special story behind it," Ruthie said in a rush of excitement. Abigail wasn't sure she had ever seen her friend so excited.

"What makes you so sure that the owner wants the box back?" Abigail asked. "Maybe they got rid of the box because some of the letters hold painful reminders of the past."

"I just have a feeling it wasn't supposed to end up in the pile of trash beside the dumpster," Ruthie says. "There is something special about this box, I just know it."

Abigail could hardly wait to see what was inside. Ruthie carefully took out the first item and laid it on the table. It was a Bible with a soft leather cover, worn from years of use. The leather was the color of milk chocolate, and Abigail knew the words inside the book were just as sweet. Inscribed on the cover was Jeremiah 29:11 "For I know the plans I have for you," declares the Lord. "Plans to prosper you and not to harm you; plans to give you hope and a future."

Abigail studied the words intently. The words of Jeremiah 29:11 brought so much hope to her; they were the words that had saved her from the pit of depression. They saved her life.

"Are you okay?" Ruthie asked.

"This verse just means so much to me," Abigail said. "It's the reason that I am alive today."

Ruthie set the Bible back on the table, gently.

"Would you like to tell me why this verse means so much to you?" Ruthie asked.

"It's a long story," Abigail said, laughing. "We might be here a while."

"That's okay," Ruthie said. "There's nothing more I'd rather do, than hear how this verse played such an important role in your life."

"Well, I guess if I tell the story, I need to start at the beginning," Abigail said as she sat down in one of the dining chairs. "It's really not the same unless you know my history."

Ruthie sat across from her friend at the table and waited patiently for her to begin her story.

"My love for people started at an early age," Abigail said. "I was the oldest of five children and spent the majority of my time helping my mother take care of my siblings. As a child, I always felt loved and accepted. Growing up, I didn't dream of having a successful career. My heart's desire was to be a wife and a mother. I was a nurturer who dreamed of having a husband to take care of and a house full of children.

"It didn't surprise my family when I decided to get married right out of high school.

"Within fifteen days of my eighteenth birthday, I graduated from high school and married Danny, my high school sweetheart. I worked several days a week arranging flowers at a local flower shop, but I always had a hot meal on the table by the time my husband got home.

"Two years after the wedding, I discovered I was pregnant. Nine months later I gave birth to my son, Mark. It wasn't long after our son was born that Danny and I started having marriage problems. I look back now and realize we got married way too young. Neither of us was mature enough to be married, let alone be parents. We both made a lot of mistakes and broke the vows we had made to one another. We divorced when I was twenty-two. I was a single mom with a two-year-old son and had no clue what I was going to do with my life. I had never wanted to be anything other than a wife and a mom.

"After the divorce, I was rejected by my church. They looked down on people who were divorced. I was so angry, and for the first time in my life I felt like nobody loved me. I began to make horrible choices, searching for love and acceptance in all the wrong places.

"I would sleep with guys I barely knew. I would feel so guilty about it and swear I'd never do it again, but they were like a drug that I couldn't live without.

"I ended up getting pregnant. I knew I wasn't equipped to be a mother of two; I could barely take care of my son.

"I walked into an abortion clinic, in need of a quick fix for my problem. The staff at the clinic told me I was making the right decision. During my appointment they told me that what was growing inside of me wasn't even considered a child yet. I replayed their description of the pregnancy over and over again in my mind, trying to justify the decision that I had made.

"When I left the abortion clinic, I was not overcome by a flood of relief. I left feeling worse than I had when I saw the two pink lines on the pregnancy test.

"I battled with an emotional pain that I had never experienced before. Fear and self-hatred led me to believe that I wasn't worth anything and no one would ever want me in their life.

"I was still working a few days a week at the local florist, trying to do anything and everything to keep from thinking about the horrible nightmare I had experienced at the abortion clinic. Every day, Satan told me what a complete failure I was. I started plotting how I could kill myself and end the emotional misery I was in.

"I know now that God had a reason for my working at the flower shop. Not only did arranging flowers and decorating bring me a small sense of joy, but He placed a very special lady in my life.

"The flower shop was owned by a local pastor's wife. She had always been very kind to me, but in the days after the abortion, she took me under her wing. I think she could sense something was terribly wrong with me.

"She invited me to go to church with her. She could tell that I was hesitant, but continued to encourage me. She said I would be accepted and loved at the church she attended. The shop owner loved me unconditionally. She is the reason I came to know the Lord as my personal savior. She taught me that I was forgiven by God and I eventually believed her, but I continued to struggle with forgiving myself.

"It wasn't long before I started dating again. I was still trying to fill the void in my heart with men, instead of allowing the Lord to fill those empty spaces that only He can fill.

"We hadn't been dating long when we decided to get married. A few months into our marriage, I realized my husband was an alcoholic. He was very abusive and extremely jealous. I sent my son, Mark, to live with his father and step-mother, because I feared for his safety. I hadn't even been married a year, when I ended up divorced again.

"My son returned to live with me after the divorce. I told myself I was going to focus on being a good mother and growing closer to the Lord, but instead I repeated my past mistakes. I jumped head-first into another abusive relationship.

"My third husband was a manipulative and controlling alcoholic. His abuse wasn't just directed towards me, but towards my son as well.

"Before I knew it, I was having suicidal thoughts again. I was convinced that the world would be a better place without me so I started planning my suicide.

"I went to work at the flower shop every day with a smile on my face. From the outside, I looked happy, but on the inside I was drowning in a sea of depression. I spent several weeks trying to decide how I would kill myself. I wrote the note and swallowed an entire bottle of pills. I lay down and waited to die. I never wanted to wake up again.

"But I did. When I woke up, my thoughts immediately turned to how I would try to kill myself the next time. I needed a plan that wouldn't fail, so I decided I would use a gun.

"After my suicide attempt, I was admitted to a mental institution where God began to show me that He valued my life.

"The owner of the local flower shop came to visit me while I was in the hospital. She brought me a card with a scripture written on it. The scripture was Jeremiah 29:11 and the words pulled me out of the pit of depression I had been in for so long."

Abigail began to recite the words. "For I know the plans I have for you, declares the Lord. Plans to prosper you and not to harm you, plans to give you hope and a future."

"I read that verse everyday and eventually started to believe it. I still read it often, because it reminds me of the horrible choices that I made and the fact that God still saved me from those choices."

You yourselves are our letter, written on our hearts, known and read by everybody. You show that you are a letter from Christ, the result of our ministry, written not with ink but with the Spirit of the living God, not on tablets of stone but on tablets of human hearts. Such confidence as this is ours through Christ before God. Not that we are competent in ourselves to claim anything for ourselves, but our competence comes from God.

2 Corinthians 3:2–5 (NIV)

chapter four

Ruthie carefully picked the Bible back up and held it in her hands. She looked at her new friend and then at the words on the book's cover. They had a completely different meaning to her now.

"Thank you for sharing your story," Ruthie said as she handed the Bible to Abigail. "I know God must have a special plan for your life."

Abigail took a deep breath as she flipped through the book. Its thin pages were yellowed, partly from age, but also from daily use. As she carefully turned the pages, several handwritten notes fell to the floor. She bent down to pick them up.

"Ruthie, this Bible is full of very special notes written to a woman named Evelyn," Abigail said.

Ruthie walked over to Abigail to see what she had discovered. Tucked in between the pages of the Bible, along with the written letters, was money.

"Look at all of this money," Ruthie exclaimed. "We need to find this woman and give this Bible back to her."

Abigail agreed.

"Ok, let's look through the Bible to see if there are any clues that could help us discover who Evelyn is," Abigail said.

Inside the front cover of the Bible, written in perfect cursive handwriting was the name Evelyn, but there was no last name. Tucked between the thin pages was letter after letter addressed to this mysterious woman. Some of the letters dated back forty-five years, but they were all written by different women.

Returning the letters didn't concern Ruthie as much as returning the money did. She knew the letters were probably important to someone, but she figured the money was even more so. Unlike the letters, the money looked new. Not dirty and heavily circulated, but crisp and fresh, the kind of bills that stuck together easily.

Ruthie laid the Bible on the table and began to take other books out of the box. Each book had money tucked between its yellowed pages.

Inside the cover of several books was a list of women's names: Katherine, Laura, Angela, Betty. The list went on and on, filling up the front and back covers of each book. The names were dated; the most recent entry was from 2009.

"Wow. I see why you were so intrigued by this box," Abigail said. "It looks like this is a list of all the women who have read these books. It's almost like a testimony of how God has used these books to impact the lives of these women."

Abigail and Ruthie continued to sift through the treasures the box held. They found a bundle of letters tied together with a pink ribbon; all of them were addressed to Evelyn.

"Have you read any of these?" Abigail asked.

"No! They seem too personal," Ruthie said.

"We may have to read them in hopes that they will lead us to the owner," Abigail said. "For now, let's continue to look at what's inside the box. We can read the letters later."

Inside the box were many more books and CD's by various Christian artists. Ruthie took two books, *Running the Red Lights* and *The Long Love Letter,* and moved them aside and discovered a black velvet bag at the very bottom of the box.

Ruthie reached into the bag and pulled out a handful of beautiful pearls. Some were loose, others were strung together to make a necklace.

"Look at these; I bet they're real," Ruthie said with a huge smile on her face. She had never owned a strand of pearls, let alone, held a handful of them in her hand.

"Ruthie, you're right. This is a very special box," Abigail said. "We really do need to find the owner so that we can return it."

Abigail had an idea. Maybe she and Ruthie needed to do a little investigating. Maybe the owner had left something else beside the dumpster that might give them a clue about who they were.

"I have an idea, Ruthie. Can you take me to the place where you found the box?" Abigail asked.

"Yes, I will take you to the dumpster," Ruthie said. "Do you have a place we can hide this? I don't think we should be carrying it around."

Abigail agreed. Carefully, the two friends put all the contents back into the box. They replaced the lid, tied the ribbons securely, and Abigail locked it in a cabinet where it would be safe.

The Lord does not look at the things man looks at. Man looks at the outward appearance, but the Lord looks at the heart.

1 Samuel 16:7 (NIV)

chapter five

Abigail climbed into Ruthie's car, packed with all of her treasures. Although she had seen Ruthie drive the tan station wagon through the alley many times, she had never been inside the car. Besides Ruthie, she wasn't sure if she had ever seen anyone inside the car.

The car was old and the paint had faded through the years, but surprisingly it still ran okay. The local tire shop kept it running and the filling station kept the gas tank full, thanks to an anonymous individual who always paid for Ruthie's gas. Nobody knew who did the good deed, but it was a blessing to Ruthie because it enabled her to continue doing what she loved. She could spend her time looking for trinkets and treasures that she could use to bless others instead of worrying about how she would pay for gas.

The items in the car weren't considered treasures to most people, but to Ruthie they served a purpose. Ruthie drove her station wagon all over town, always ready to give away the items inside to someone in desperate need of them. If she saw a child in need of a pair of shoes, you could guarantee Ruthie had the perfect size tucked away somewhere in her car.

Abigail knew if they took Ruthie's car to the dumpster, where she had discovered the box, no one would question what they were doing. It wasn't unusual for Ruthie to drive through the alley picking up items to add to her collection. On many occasions Abigail benefited from Ruthie's discoveries. Ruthie had a keen eye when it came to finding things that Abigail could refurbish. She was always looking for a special piece of furniture for Abigail's next project.

Driving down the alley, Abigail felt ashamed of the many times she had felt sorry for Ruthie when she saw her driving around in the beat-up station wagon. It wasn't until that moment in the car that Abigail realized how much she could learn from Ruthie's generosity and the simple life that she chose to live.

The women headed south to the newer part of town. Ruthie pulled up next to a dumpster and parked the car.

"This is where I found the box," Ruthie said proudly. "There was nothing inside the dumpster, but sitting beside it was a pile of trash. I started to rummage through it and my eye caught something green. That's when I discovered it."

Abigail chuckled at Ruthie as she described her big find. She got out of the car, walked over to the dumpster, and lifted the lid to look inside. Empty. The pile of trash was still sitting next to the dumpster but it looked to be only old newspapers and empty soda cans and bottles.

Abigail noticed a house a few yards from the dumpster, but it was vacant. She wondered if the owner of the box had lived there at one time. It seemed strange that someone would pick a random dumpster to leave a box full of so many treasured memories.

Abigail and Ruthie stood in silence. So many questions swirled through Abigail's mind. Who in the world was Evelyn? Did she leave the box next to the dumpster or did someone else? What were she and Ruthie supposed to do with the box?

"Let's go back to the shop and collect our thoughts," Abigail said. "I could use a glass of tea, and I think it might be time to read those letters."

Abigail and Ruthie sat down at the dining table with a cold glass of tea and the box that held so much mystery.

They sifted through its contents, searching for any clues that could lead them to Evelyn.

Ruthie carefully took out the stack of letters that were tied together with the pink satin ribbon. She unfolded a single sheet of tear-stained paper, fragile from being opened and read so many times.

"This letter isn't written to Evelyn," Ruthie said. "Evelyn wrote this letter to a girl named Hannah."

Abigail took the letter from Ruthie and began to read the words out loud, hoping it would give them some insight into who Evelyn was.

Dearest Hannah,

Today as I visited you in jail, you seemed so much better than the last time we spoke. I enjoy our time together immensely and you are in my prayers continually. I pray the Lord will give you the strength and power to overcome your addiction to drugs and any other strongholds that you are facing. I pray that God's love will transform your life in a way that will keep you from hurting anyone ever again. I pray you will have an overwhelming desire to experience God's love for you, to desire His word and to hide it in your heart. I pray in your moments of weakness, God will provide all you need to resist the temptations of this world. May His peace fill your heart and may you always feel His presence. I love you and look forward to what God has in store for your future. Always remember Jeremiah 29:11–13. God has a plan for your life!

With Love,

Evelyn

When Abigail had finished reading the letter, Ruthie took another one from the stack and began to read:

Dearest Hannah,

As your court date quickly approaches, I pray that the Lord's favor will be upon you. God knows your heart and the changes you have made. His word says that 'the Lord does not look at the outward appearance like man does, but at the heart.' I will continue to keep you in my prayers. May you rest in God's promises.

Love,

Evelyn

Abigail opened the last letter.

"Look, Ruthie, this letter is from Hannah." Abigail said.

Dear Evelyn,

Thank you for your support. I am not sure I have the right words to express my appreciation for all that you have done for me. Thank you so much for the encouraging books, letters, and for your prayers. I will be going to court on July 15th. Last night I found out that when I am released from jail, I'll be homeless. I have been disqualified from living in the low-income apartment complex that I was living in before I went to jail. I'm not sure what's going to happen. Most of the places around here are way out of my price range. The places that I can afford to rent are not big enough for my family. I know deep in my heart that the Lord will provide for my family, but right now I feel so helpless. Sorry to bother you with all of my worries. I had to get some of them off my chest and I knew you were the one person who would understand. I have been praying about everything but I'm still nervous and afraid. Thanks for listening.

Love,

Hannah

Just as Abigail and Ruthie had finished the letters, Mimsey walked in. Ruthie quickly put the letters back in the box and replaced the lid.

Mimsey had frequented the shop, but Abigail still hadn't formed a very close friendship with her. She always seemed to hold Abigail at arm's length, afraid to get too close.

"Hey, Mimsey, how are you on this beautiful day?" Abigail asked as Mimsey took a seat at the table. Abigail got up, poured Mimsey a glass of tea, and rejoined the ladies.

"Just what are you two doing?" Mimsey asked with a suspicious tone. Her eyes kept darting over to the box that was lying on the table.

"Did I see the two of you driving through the alley earlier in Ruthie's car? I've never seen anyone ride with you, Ruthie, what's the special occasion?"

Ruthie stood up, suddenly very nervous. She took the box and headed towards the back door.

"I've got to go now," she said, giving Abigail a strange look. Before Abigail could stop her, Ruthie was gone.

"What was that all about?" Mimsey seemed surprised by Ruthie's sudden escape. "Does Ruthie not like me?"

"I don't think that's it, Mimsey. Ruthie's just shy and it takes her a while to warm up to people."

"Tell me more about her," Mimsey asked, genuinely interested. "It seems like you two are really good friends. I want to get to know Ruthie better, but she doesn't seem to want to get to know me."

"Ruthie's a very private person," Abigail said. "Even I don't know a whole lot about her. I do know that she is an incredible person who loves the Lord with all of her heart. I really admire that about her."

"So why were the two of you in her car?" Mimsey asked. "I can't believe you even got in there with all that stuff. What's in that box that Ruthie had?"

Abigail liked Mimsey, but sometimes she was so nosey. Her curiosity was killing her and she would do just about anything to find out the secret Abigail and Ruthie shared.

"Mims, it's no big deal," Abigail said. "Ruthie needs my help with a project she's working on. I'm not sure she wants anyone to know about it yet, so I need to respect her privacy."

"Were you and Ruthie out looking for more items to redo?" Mimsey couldn't handle not knowing what Ruthie and Abigail were up to.

"All I can say is that God brought Ruthie into my life so that I can help her with a special project," Abigail said.

"Huh," Mimsey said, obviously annoyed.

"Be patient, Mims, I'm sure Ruthie will warm up to you," Abigail said.

Mimsey wasn't really concerned about whether Ruthie would ever warm up to her. She just wanted to know what was in the box and why her friends were keeping secrets.

Therefore go and make disciples of all nations, baptizing them in the name of the Father and of the Son and of the Holy Spirit, and teaching them to obey everything I have commanded you. And surely I am with you always, to the very end of the age.

Matthew 28:19–20 (NIV)

chapter six

The next morning Ruthie showed up at Abigail's door with the box tucked securely under her arm.

"Hey, Ruthie," Abigail said as she opened the door. "Why in the world did you leave here in such a hurry yesterday?"

"I didn't want Mimsey to know about our secret," Ruthie said. "I see the way she looks at me. I know she thinks I'm crazy, driving through alleys and picking up what she considers junk. I don't think she would understand the sentiments of the box."

Abigail knew there was tension between Ruthie and Mimsey. They were two very different women. Ruthie was reserved; Mimsey was nosey and opinionated. Ruthie was content with the simple things in life. As long as she had clothes on her back and a roof over her head, she was satisfied.

Mimsey, on the other hand, was always dressed in the latest fashions. She didn't intend to give off the impression that material things were a priority, but to people who didn't know her well it seemed that material things were all that mattered to Mimsey.

After Abigail's visit with Mimsey the day before, she knew her friend desired to get to know Ruthie.

"Ruthie, I think if you would just give Mimsey a chance, you would see that she's not as stuck-up and materialistic as you think," Abigail said. "What if we could use the box to share the love of Jesus with Mimsey?

"You know she doesn't like to hear us talk about Jesus, but if she helped us find the owner of the box and read some of its contents, maybe God could soften Mimsey's heart."

Ruthie knew Abigail was right. She had spent too much time judging Mimsey and the way she chose to live her life and not enough time sharing God's love with her.

"I think you're right," Ruthie said. "This could be just the opportunity Mimsey needs to hear about the love of Christ. Maybe these letters and books will show her just how much God cares about her. But I think it's still too soon to let her in on the secret."

"Why don't we finish looking through the box," Abigail said. "We can call Mimsey after we have a better idea of what we're dealing with."

- -

Ruthie and Abigail sat side-by-side on the antique sofa, excited to see the additional treasures they would find inside the box.

"I think we should start going through the books," Ruthie said. "There must be an explanation for all the money. It makes me nervous and even a little bit guilty to have all this money here that doesn't belong to us."

"There's no need for us to feel guilty about the money," Abigail said looking at her friend. "We haven't done anything wrong and we intend to return it. We just need to pray that God will guide us through this crazy predicament that we are in. I know He will open the right doors for us. You just wait and see."

Abigail and Ruthie started flipping through the yellowed pages of the books.

"We need some sort of plan on how to go through all of these books," Ruthie said. "I don't think we should take the money out of the books to count it. What if there's a reason why each book has a certain amount?"

"That's probably a good idea," Abigail said.

The women started with a small blue paperback book that was at the top of the stack. They searched through *The Greatest Miracle in the World* by Og Mandino and discovered a hundred dollar bill stuck in-between every couple of pages.

"This is so much money," Ruthie exclaimed, her eyes wide at the sight of the hundred dollar bill. "What will we do if we can't find the owner of the box?"

"I think we each need to take a book, look through them and take notes about what we find and how much money is in each one," Abigail said.

Abigail picked up another small book called *The Practice of the Presence of God,* only to discover that it, too, had hundred dollar bills stuck between many of its pages. It also had a list of names written on the front and back cover–most likely the names of the women who had read the book.

Ruthie seemed concerned. "Don't you think it's going to take us a long time to go through all these books? It will delay us finding the owner and giving the money back."

"I think we can start by skimming the books," Abigail said. "If that's not what we are supposed to do, God will show us the next step."

"Let's count the money in each book and write the amounts down in a notebook," Ruthie said.

"Wonderful idea," Abigail said as she grabbed a notebook and pen.

Ruthie began to name each book and the amount of money that each one held. As she called out the amounts, Abigail wrote them down in the notebook.

"*The Greatest Miracle in the World*," Ruthie said. "Wow! There's seven hundred dollars in this book."

Abigail took a tiny book and thumbed through its pages, finding seventy dollars.

"*The Long Love Letter*," Ruthie said, counting another hundred dollars.

"This one is titled *Same Kind of Different as Me*," Abigail said. "You are not going to believe this. There's a thousand dollars in this book."

The women continued to go through each book, counting the money and logging the totals into the notebook. When they were finished they had counted $40,000.

"Why in the world would someone leave that much money in a pile of trash?" Abigail asked, completely shocked by the grand total.

"This is so much money," Ruthie said as she paced back in forth in front of Abigail. Abigail could tell she was even more nervous about the money now that they knew how much there was.

"I think you should lock it back up so that it's safe," Ruthie said.

Abigail took the box back to the library and locked it up. Ruthie agreed to come back the following day so they could decide what their next step would be to solving the mystery.

Love the Lord your God with all your heart and with all your soul and with all your strength and with all your mind.

Luke 10:27 (NIV)

chapter seven

Abigail and Ruthie met again the following day. They sat on the antique sofa in Abigail's shop with the box resting on the cushions between them. They had each spent the previous night skimming through the books, hoping something they read would lead them to Evelyn.

"Ruthie, did you find anything interesting in your book?" Abigail was ready to get to the bottom of the mystery.

"I found something interesting, but nothing that gets us any closer to finding the owner of the box," Ruthie said, as she thumbed through the pages of a book. "I did learn that God considers us to be the greatest miracle in the world. He has placed more than a hundred million receptors in the human eye so that we can enjoy the blessing of His creation through sight.

"It says here that each of us has twenty-four thousand fibers in each one of our ears so that we can experience the sound of the wind in the trees, the ocean tide sweeping across rocks, the majesty of an opera, a robin's plea, the squeal and delight of children playing," Ruthie read in awe. "The Lord gave us our senses to bless us."

"Wow, I guess I've never taken the time to think about all the blessings that God gives us through His creation," Abigail said. "Sounds like a really great book, Ruthie."

"The best thing about the book is that it tells the story of a rag picker," Ruthie said. "I'm a rag picker, Abi, did you know that?"

"What exactly is a rag picker?" Abigail asked as she stood up from the sofa. She walked over to the tea pot in the dining room and poured two cups. She handed Ruthie her tea, with two cubes of sugar, just the way she liked it.

"I'm a rag picker because I make my living scavenging for rejected items that you might be able to restore or for items that other people might be able to use," Ruthie said.

"Abi, for you to really understand my reason for being a rag picker, I guess it's finally time for me to share the story of how I became one."

"I would love it if you would share your story with me," Abigail said. She was humbled that Ruthie felt comfortable enough to finally tell her why she chose to live the way she did. Abigail was about to discover a new depth to Ruthie. She was finally going to break past the surface level.

"No one has ever asked me to share my story before," Ruthie said. "I've kept it to myself all of these years, but I think God wants me to share it with you."

- -

Ruthie warmed their cups of tea as Abigail sat, patiently waiting for her to finally open up to her and reveal who she truly was. Abigail listened as Ruthie began to share her life story.

"I was married to a handsome soldier named Jack Jones," Ruthie began. "Four months after we were married, Jack was sent off to war. Shortly after

Patty Bultman

he left, I discovered that I was pregnant. I wrote
Jack a letter to tell him the good news and he was
thrilled that he was going to be a father. I was four
months pregnant when the dreaded knock on the
door came. Two men in uniform came to tell me
that Jack had been killed in the war. My heart was
so broken. We had loved each other with such pas-
sion. I didn't know how I would ever live without
him. I battled with depression for several months
after his death, but I knew I had to find a way to
pull myself together because I was going to be a
mother.

"About five months after Jack's death, I gave
birth to a beautiful baby girl, whom I named
Margaret. I was a young widow and a new mother
and was scared to death. I had no idea how to raise a
child on my own. I didn't have any family members
who could help me. My parents had been killed in
a car accident when I was in college, just a few years
before Jack and I were married.

"I had always dreamed of using my life to serve
the Lord. I had felt God's calling to go into ministry
early on in my life, but I quit Bible College after my
parents' death and never had the courage to enroll

in another school. After Jack died and the baby was born, I decided to move back here where I had been raised. To make ends meet, I worked at the local motel cleaning rooms and then cleaned two houses for additional money. One of the houses I cleaned was this one," Ruthie said as she pointed around Abigail's shop.

"At the time a woman named Hope Pettigrew lived here. As a matter of fact, Hope is the one who gave me my house and this coat," Ruthie said. "She loved the color green, so much that she kept this house painted green during the years she lived here. I loved Hope. I cleaned her house for twenty years. My daughter, Margaret, spent a lot of time here too. Hope would let her sit at the kitchen table and they would practice their dinner manners. Hope taught Margaret how to be a sweet and proper young lady. They would have tea parties and drink tea from china cups and eat shortbread cookies. I can just picture Margaret's tiny little finger sticking out as she sipped the tea." Ruthie smiled.

"My sweet Margaret grew up quickly. She was so beautiful and all the boys liked her. I had big dreams for my daughter, but the one thing I did not want was for her to fall in love with a soldier. I couldn't bear the thought of her losing the love of her life the way I had.

"Margaret eventually met a man named James Stokes. Thankfully he wasn't a soldier. The two met at a political event that Margaret had helped cater. It wasn't long before James was head-over-heels in love with Margaret. They ended up eloping in Las Vegas. I know that was never my daughter's dream. She desired to have the big, beautiful wedding that every bride dreams of. She wanted a lavish wedding dress fit for a princess. Instead, she settled for her best church dress and no guests. After the wedding, Margaret and James moved to Chicago, but we talked often. A few months after she moved, I started to notice something different in her voice. She wasn't happy and full of life like she had been. She was losing her joy. I worried about her constantly and asked if she would come home to visit me for my birthday. I was hoping she would come alone so that I could talk to her about what was bothering her. She called to tell me she was coming home. It had been a year since I had seen her."

Ruthie began to cry, but choked back the tears to continue.

"When I saw her get off the plane I couldn't believe I was looking at my daughter. She had lost so much weight. She looked very sick and had bruises all over her body. I got a sick feeling in my stomach; I knew that her husband was beating her. She tried to cover it up, but she was a lousy liar. Besides, bruises don't lie.

"I had cleaned some extra houses and had saved money so that the two of us could go out for a nice dinner. When I mentioned it to her she said she would rather go home and have pancakes. She wanted me to fix her pancakes in the shape of an "M" the way I did when she was a little girl. The special pancakes had always made her smile. As we were eating, we talked and laughed. I got the impression that she wanted to tell me something. Margaret had volunteered at a shelter for women. Her job was to pray with them and she was privileged to do so. She felt like the job at the shelter was her way of being Jesus' hands and feet. She fell in love with every woman she met and often cried for and with them as they shared their painful stories.

"That night as we were eating our pancakes, Margaret told me she was no longer working at the women's shelter. I couldn't believe what my daughter was telling me. She loved working with the women. I couldn't think of a single reason why she would want to stop working there.

"Through her tears, she told me that James wanted her to be at home more, that he wanted all of her attention for himself. She stopped working to try and make him happy, but he was never home.

"By this time Margret and I were both crying and I was terrified for my daughter's safety. My motherly instinct kicked in and I told her that there was no way she could go back to Chicago where he could hurt her. I wouldn't allow it.

"My daughter, my baby girl, said if she didn't go back home, James would find her and kill her.

"That he had already held a gun to her head and threatened to take her life. The police came and arrested him, but he was quickly released. He had been furious with her for letting the police take him to jail."

About that time, the sound of the front bell signaled that a customer had arrived.

"I'm so sorry Ruthie," Abigail said as she squeezed Ruthie's shoulder. "I'll be right back and you can finish your story."

Ruthie tried to regain her composure as she waited for Abigail to finish helping her customer.

In just a few minutes Abigail rejoined her friend and nodded her head for her to continue.

"Margaret told me she would go back to Chicago and pray for her husband. I knew that wasn't a good idea, but she wouldn't listen to me.

"I begged and pleaded for her to stay with me, to get a fresh start. I promised to protect her. I think I was angry enough to kill James. I couldn't understand why the Lord would allow my daughter to be in such a dangerous situation.

"Margaret thought that if she went home, prayed for her husband, and was submissive to him, everything would turn out okay. I tried to explain to her that Biblical submission never included abuse.

"During the next few days, I dreaded the moment Margaret would step on the plane and fly back to Chicago. I was so fearful for my daughter, but through the fear, I heard the Lord reminding me, Fear not! But I didn't listen to Him. How could I push my fears aside during a time like that?

"The day I took her to the airport I pleaded with her, once again, to stay. I told her it wasn't too late for her to change her mind. I wanted her to stay so badly. She didn't. I walked her into the airport, then went to the car and wept.

Ruthie paused for a moment, looked into Abigail's eyes, and said, "Please bear with me; this is the hardest part of the story." Abigail grabbed her hand and held it as she continued.

"Margaret called me every day and assured me that everything was okay. She was even planning to go back to work at the shelter.

"About two weeks after she had returned to Chicago, she called me and asked if I could meet her at the airport. She said she would explain when she was safe with me. I prayed the entire way, thanking God that my daughter would be safe once she got home. When she got in the car, she said the violence had gotten worse and she was beginning to fear for her life. I was so happy to see her. I thanked God all the way home that she was with me.

"I didn't sleep for several nights after Margaret returned home. She was having nightmares, crying in her sleep. We would sit on the couch and she would put her head in my lap as I smoothed her hair in an attempt to soothe her. About a week after Margaret returned home, I heard a car pull up outside of our house at about 4 a.m. I heard the car door slam, followed by footsteps on the porch and pounding on the door. Margaret woke up terrified. She screamed for me to call the police, as James busted through the door.

"He started yelling at Margaret. Telling her how stupid she was and how we were both going to have to pay for her disobedience. He pulled a gun from his coat and started waving it at me and swearing. I ran into the bedroom, slammed the door, locked it and reached for the phone. He was kicking the door with such force that I knew it wouldn't hold. As he busted the door open, I was face to face with the barrel of his gun. He just laughed. He began to tell me how he had raped and abused my daughter. Then he told me how he was going to kill me. The way he laughed made my skin crawl. I imagined his laugh sounding like the devil's.

"About that time, Margaret stepped behind him and tried to push him down. It startled him but he didn't lose his balance. He turned around, pointed the gun at her, and shot her in the face. I was in such complete shock from just seeing my daughter get shot that I almost didn't feel the bullet hit my arm. I had heard the gun go off a second time, but all I could concentrate on was the blood coming from Margaret's limp, lifeless body. Before I knew what was happening, James put the gun to his own head and pulled the trigger. After that, I was completely numb."

Ruthie took a deep breath and continued.

"After the murder/suicide, I went into a deep depression. There was no way I could continue to live in the house. Every time I closed my eyes I saw my daughter's body in a pool of blood. I ended up sleeping on the streets for months. I was so lost in a sea of depression and sadness that I had no idea what I was going to do. I was mad at God. Anger boiled inside of me.

"One day a woman saw me over by the gas station. She pulled up beside me, rolled the window down, and handed me a book. She said that God had told her I needed to read it. Just as soon as she handed it to me, she was gone. Up until that time in my life my favorite book had always been the Bible, but I couldn't even bring myself to open it. The book the lady gave me was called *The Shack* by William P. Young. I read the book and it changed my life. I started trusting God again."

Abigail had never seen Ruthie cry so hard. She had confessed her deepest heartache and her heart broke for her friend. Now she understood why Ruthie chose to live the way she did, why she loved to help women who had been hurt and abused.

"There was something about the book that I could really relate to," Ruthie explained.

From memory Ruthie began to recite a section of the book.

"Evil is a word we use to describe the absence of Good, just as the word darkness is described as the absence of Light or death to describe the absence of Life. Both evil and darkness can only be understood in relation to light and good; they do not have any actual existence. I am Light and I am Good. I am Love and there is no darkness in me. Light and good actually exist. So removing yourself from me (talking about God, Jesus and the Holy Spirit) will plunge you into darkness. Declaring independence will result in evil, because apart from me, you can only draw upon yourself. That is death, because you have separated yourself from me, which is Life.

"After reading that, I knew I had plunged myself into darkness and it was killing me little by little. I had turned my back on God but He had not turned His back on me. I continued to read and my eyes were opened even more as I read about God's great love for me. How He does not want a single one of His children to perish. He wants us to accept His love. God loves us but will not tolerate sin. We must ask for forgiveness and mercy. At that moment, I changed my attitude toward my circumstances. I knew Jesus loved me and I decided I would use the brokenness of my past to help change the world, one woman at a time. Jesus commanded that we are to 'Love the Lord our God with all our heart and with all our soul and with all of our mind. This is the greatest commandment. And the second is this: Love your neighbor as yourself."

Ruthie quoted scripture beautifully and Abigail loved to hear the Word of God flow from her mouth.

"So that is why you live in that tiny little house and commit to doing God's work every day?" Abigail asked.

"I was very fortunate that Hope gave me the shed to live in," Ruthie said. "She was a living testimony of God's commandment to love your neighbor as yourself."

"Ruthie, I'm so sorry you had to go through so much pain. God has definitely used the pain of your past for His glory." Abigail hugged her friend. It wasn't often that Ruthie allowed hugs, but this time she didn't pull away.

He will cover you with his feathers, and under his wings you will find refuge; his faithfulness will be your shield and rampart.

Psalm 91:4 (NIV)

chapter eight

A few days after Ruthie had shared her story with Abigail, the two friends were sitting at the dining table in Abigail's shop, a plate of blueberry muffins between them.

The bells on the front door jingled as they ate the warm muffins and sipped hot tea. Mimsey greeted them with a warm smile and sat down next to them at the dining table.

"Good morning, Mimsey," Ruthie said as she handed her a steaming cup of tea and a warm muffin.

Abigail couldn't help but notice Ruthie's sudden change of heart towards Mimsey. She must have remembered that God wanted her to share His love with other women. Abigail and Ruthie both knew that if anyone needed to experience God's incredible love, it was Mimsey.

As Mimsey was sipping her tea, she suddenly noticed something familiar sitting on the table.

"Hey, where did you get that box?" Mimsey asked. "I used to have one just like that, but I used it recently to deliver a meal to a lady who is renting one of my houses."

Ruthie and Abigail looked at each other, excitement written all over their faces.

"What part of town does the renter live in?" Ruthie asked with urgency.

"The renter is Mrs. White and she lives in the north part of town." Mimsey said.

"I know Mrs. White," Ruthie said. "I share my lunch from the diner with her every day. While she eats, we talk about God and His Word."

Abigail couldn't help but notice how God was working to strengthen the relationship between Ruthie and Mimsey. Ruthie had been so hesitant to let Mimsey in on their secret, but now she was talking non-stop about how she discovered the box. She told Mimsey all about the books, the letters, the velvet bag full of pearls, and the worn Bible.

"It's not the books and stuff that have us curious," Ruthie said. "It's all the money we found tucked between the pages of the books."

"There was money stuck between the pages of all the books?" Mimsey asked, a look of sheer surprise on her face. "What dumpster was it next to? Were there houses nearby?"

Ruthie and Abigail smiled at each other. Mimsey couldn't contain her excitement. It was obvious just how much she enjoyed being included in their secret.

"Mims, we went to the dumpster the day that Ruthie found the box, but we didn't find any clues to who the owner is," Abigail said. "The house next to the dumpster was vacant, so we came back here and started going through the box hoping that we would find some clues. It's become a pretty big mystery."

"Mimsey, do you think there's any way Mrs. White could have left the box by the dumpster?" Ruthie asked.

"I guess it's possible," Mimsey said. "I can ask her if she still has the box I gave her. Would you mind if I looked in it?" she asked, curiosity all across her face.

Ruthie carefully untied the ribbons and lifted the lid. Mimsey began to rummage through the box, pulling out many of the books and placing them on the table.

Suddenly, with a book in each hand, Mimsey stopped what she was doing. She looked at her friends and smiled.

"This was the project you were working on the day I saw you two driving through the alley in Ruthie's car?"

Abigail winked at Ruthie as Mimsey continued to dig through the treasures inside the box. Something suddenly caught Mimsey's eye and she put down the books that she had been holding in her hand.

She took the black velvet bag from the box, opened it, and poured the beautiful pearls into the palm of her hand. She had never seen so many pearls—all so precious. Mimsey stuck her hand back into the bag and felt a piece of paper. She pulled it out and showed it to her friends.

"Hey, did either of you notice this letter with the pearls?" Mimsey asked as she unfolded the faded piece of paper.

"Read it," Ruthie said. "Maybe it's the story behind the pearls."

Dear Evelyn,

Thank you so much for organizing the Purity Retreat that my daughter Lila and I recently attended. Our lives have been forever changed.

When Lila and I were first invited to go to the retreat, I had no intention of attending and I really didn't want my daughter to go either. Why would I want to go to a purity retreat? There was nothing pure about me. I was molested by my uncle when I was five years old and the abuse continued for six years.

In high school, I slept with my boyfriend because I wanted to feel loved. I was desperately trying to erase all the bad memories associated with my childhood. It wasn't long before I ended up pregnant. My boyfriend told his mom and she took me to an abortion clinic. She said I had to have an abortion because her son was too young to be a father and a child would make her family look bad.

The guilt from the abortion and the scars from my childhood were too much for me to handle. I started drinking shortly after the abortion. When I was drunk, I didn't have to think about my problems.

One night while I was at the bar, an older guy bought me several drinks. I ended up leaving with him. I was lonely and desperately needed to feel loved. We slept together and I ended up pregnant again.

There was no way I would have another abortion. I barely survived the first one. I decided to quit school, get a job, and raise my baby. Nine months later I had a beautiful baby girl that I named Lila.

When Lila was in elementary school she started to attend a program at a local church called Awanas. Lila began to learn about God and the Bible. She would come home and recite her memory verses for me or sing cute little Bible songs that she had learned. On the nights Lila was at the church, I went to the bar. When the church bus would bring Lila home I was usually passed out on the couch in a drunken slumber.

I spent most of Lila's childhood addicted to alcohol, trying to find love and acceptance in the arms of all the wrong men. I finally sobered up when she was in high school but had never given my life to Jesus. I really had no intentions of going to the purity retreat with my daughter. I had never felt welcome at church. I always felt like people were staring at the invisible scarlet letter on my chest.

As the retreat grew closer, I knew it would break my daughter's heart if I didn't go with her. I still wasn't sure how I could sit and listen to a Bible study on purity with my past hanging over my head.

For some reason, one of the verses Lila had so often recited kept coming to my mind. It was Psalm 91:4 "He will cover you with his feathers, and under his wings you will find refuge; his faithfulness will be your shield and rampart."

It started to become a habit for me to look around and see if I could find a feather. Each time I found one, it was like God was reminding me that He was watching over me. Could He really care for me that much?

Lila came home after the first night of the retreat about to burst with excitement. She told me about the white wedding dress that had been on display as a symbol of purity and how sin tarnishes and stains our purity. She told me that as they talked about sin, they used spray paint to destroy the dress, to represent how sin can tarnish something beautiful.

Then they talked about how God sent Jesus to take away our sin, and how He makes us spotless and as white as snow. Lila told me about asking Jesus for forgiveness and making Him the number one man in our lives. Lila was so passionate about her relationship with Jesus. She had such a deep understanding of this God I didn't know.

Then she told me something I will never forget. She said, "Mom I don't have an earthly father but I have an amazing Heavenly Father that can forgive you of all your sins." She cried. She began to share the love of God with me and I accepted Jesus as my personal savior that very night. It was the most freeing moment of my life. Every burden I had been carrying for all those years, I lay at the foot of the cross. Lila and I prayed together, tears of joy streaming down our faces.

Saturday night we went to the mother/daughter segment of the retreat. When we walked into the event center it looked like we had arrived at our dream wedding. It was breathtakingly beautiful. There were candles everywhere and the most extravagant wedding cake I had ever seen.

We were served a delicious feast fit for a princess and then a woman shared her story of purity. She was thirty years old and still a virgin. She cried as she talked about how hard it was to be lonely and to watch her friends get married and have kids. But she knew God would provide her prince in His perfect timing. She compared her life of purity to a pearl. She described an oyster getting a grain of sand in it. It gets irritated and tries to get rid of the irritation by spinning layers of blood over the piece of sand, until it forms a pearl.

She said that God values pearls so highly that He mentions them in the Bible several times. Despite our ugly sin, God sent His one and only Son to die on the cross for us. His blood covers all of our sins.

Saturday night was just a glimpse of what God has to offer His children. Thank you so much for being obedient to God and for sharing His love with people like me.

In Him,

Kim

"What an incredible story of God's amazing grace," Abigail exclaimed. "I will never look at a pearl the same way again."

As Abigail placed the pearls and letter back into the bag, Mimsey took the worn Bible out of the box.

"Oh…this is a treasure," she said as she breathed in a heavy sigh. "Why would anyone throw this away?"

"Mimsey, we don't think the box was thrown away on purpose," Abigail said. "Ruthie and I believe it was put there for a purpose. The owner wanted someone to find it."

"Well, I guess I never looked at it that way," Mimsey said. "But what would be the purpose of leaving it in a pile of trash for someone to find? It seems to me like the mystery surrounding this box is just getting bigger and bigger."

Abigail and Ruthie agreed. They were finding more and more clues, but not coming up with any answers.

Abigail stood up from the table. "I hate to be a party pooper, but I have a lot of work to do. This mystery has been consuming so much of my time that I haven't accomplished much around the shop. What if we continue our conversation tomorrow, over lunch at the Darling Diner?"

"That sounds great," Mimsey said. "Maybe the food will shed some light on the mystery."

Therefore, if anyone is in Christ, he is a new creation; the old has gone, the new has come.

2 Corinthians 5:17 (NIV)

chapter nine

Later that evening, the bell on the front door jingled letting Abigail know she had a visitor. Each time she heard the bell, she thought about an old saying she had heard long ago. "Every time a bell rings, another angel gets her wings." Abigail looked up from the chair she was sanding to see a familiar face.

She smiled. "Hey, Mimsey, what brings you by again today?"

"I need to talk to you about your insurance," Mimsey said in an awkward voice. "I forgot to mention it when I was here earlier."

Abigail wasn't buying Mimsey's reason for the unexpected visit. She could tell by Mimsey's voice and body language that something was heavy on her heart.

"How about we go sit on the porch with a glass of iced tea and chat," Abigail asked. "I could use a break from my latest project." She pointed to the chair she had been sanding for several hours. It had been a gift from Ruthie and she had almost finished stripping all of the faded green paint from the wood. She planned to paint the straight-backed chair a vibrant cherry red.

Abigail grabbed two glasses and filled them with ice and raspberry tea. She took a small plate and placed a couple of sugar cookies on it. She had a sneaking suspicion that the conversation she was about to have would be easier with a sweet treat.

Abigail walked out to the porch, but before she could even sit down, Mimsey started talking a mile-a-minute about her insurance policy.

"Mims, you're the best insurance agent a girl could have, but I know you didn't stop by to talk about my policy," Abigail said as she reached for Mimsey's hand.

Tears welled up in Mimsey's eyes.

"You know me too well," Mimsey said as she stood up and started to pace around the porch. "Do you think we could go back inside to talk?"

Mimsey was so serious that Abigail wasn't sure what to expect from their conversation. She stood up, took Mimsey by the hand, and led her back into the shop. She motioned for Mimsey to take a seat at the table and placed the iced tea and cookies in front of her. Abigail walked over and hung the closed sign on the front door and rejoined her friend.

"Abigail, you have to promise not to tell anyone about this."

"I promise, Mims. What we talk about is between you and me. It won't leave this room."

"I've been hanging on to a secret for years and it's tearing me up inside," Mimsey said as she nervously played with her tea glass. "It all started when I was in college looking for Mr. Right. I dated a few guys before meeting Jim and ended up pregnant. I panicked and had an abortion right away."

Tears were falling down Mimsey's face, as she finally revealed the secret that she had carried around for so long.

"Back then they didn't tell you it was a baby," she said. "Shortly after Jim and I got married, I discovered that I would never be able to have children.

The doctor asked me if I had been pregnant before and I lied."

Abigail squeezed Mimsey's hand.

"Take a deep breath," Abigail said. She knew that Mimsey was sharing a dark secret from her past that was long overdue. "Take your time. There's no rush. I'm here to listen."

Mimsey took a deep breath, wiped the tears off her face, and continued. "Having the abortion messed me up for life," she said. "I thought it was only because I couldn't have children, but it's more than that. The guilt has just consumed me, and I can't live with myself anymore. I've been living a lie for so many years.

"I have tried everything to numb the pain but I can't keep pretending that the abortion never happened," Mimsey said as she wrung her hands nervously. "I had to tell someone, and you are the only person I trust.

"When Jim and I realized that we would never be able to have children, we decided we would adopt a child," Mimsey continued. "We had just started the adoption process when Jim got a call from an old high-school girlfriend. She told Jim that he had a five-year-old son and she needed him to raise the little boy because she was dying. I'm sure you can imagine what a complete shock it was for Jim and me to find out that he had a son. We didn't hesitate to take the little boy and raise him as our own."

Abigail knew that Mimsey had a son who was in college, but she just assumed, as did most of the people in town, that he had been adopted by Mimsey and her husband when he was a young boy. She never would have guessed that Chad was actually Jim's biological son.

"Chad always felt loved and never thought being adopted was a bad thing," Mimsey said. "He never questioned the adoption, until recently. He's attending medical school and had to do a project on DNA. He wanted to test Jim's DNA for his project. We never dreamed he would compare Jim's DNA to his own, but he did. Now he knows that Jim is his biological father. He wants to know the whole story." Mimsey blew her nose and wiped her eyes.

"Abigail, help me! I feel like this is my opportunity to tell the truth about everything, but I am so afraid I'll hurt all the people who I've betrayed," Mimsey said, helplessness filled her voice.

"Mimsey, all you have to do is give all of these heavy burdens to Jesus," Abigail said. "Believe that Jesus died on the cross for your sins. Believe the Bible and all that it says, because it is the truth that will set you free."

"But how do I give my burdens to Jesus?" Mimsey asked.

"Make the decision to have a relationship with Jesus and He will guide and direct your paths," Abigail said. "He is a forgiving God. He will forgive the abortion and all of your other sins. If you accept that forgiveness, He will remember your sins no more. All you have to do is ask."

Abigail was crying now. The story that Mimsey had shared touched a raw place inside of her. She had lived out a story similar to Mimsey's. At times the pain was still so real, but she knew she was forgiven. She knew there was healing in the name of Jesus.

"Want to know a secret, Mims?"

Mimsey looked at Abigail, interested to hear what her friend had to say. She couldn't imagine

Abigail having a secret as scandalous and shameful as hers.

"Jesus healed me from a sinful past," Abigail said. "He forgave me for having an abortion and he replaced the guilt and pain with peace and hope."

Mimsey stared at her speechless. She couldn't believe that another person could comprehend the kind of pain and guilt she had been hiding for so many years.

"The guilt and pain that I had after my abortion caused me to go into a deep depression," Abigail continued. "I was so depressed that I tried to take my life. Thankfully, by the grace of God, He lifted me out of the pit. He restored me, gave me hope."

"Mimsey, He can do the same for you," Abigail said as she put her arm around her friend. "Please accept His precious gift. It's the best decision I've ever made."

"I do want that, Abigail. I can't go on living like this. Would you please pray with me," Mimsey pleaded. "I want a relationship with Jesus. Teach me to love Jesus the way you do."

Abigail took Mimsey's hand and through tears she led her friend in the sinner's prayer. She listened as Mimsey prayed for forgiveness and salvation, pouring her heart out to the Lord.

What a glorious day it was. Not just for Mimsey, but for Abigail, too. Mimsey was finally free from the past that had haunted her for so long.

"Now what do I do?" Mimsey asked.

"God has a lot He wants to teach you," Abigail said. "He will guide you as you develop a relationship with Him. The Bible promises that if we draw near to God, He will draw near to us. Do you have a Bible?"

Abigail was so excited to get Mimsey into God's word, where she would learn all about His abundant love for her.

"I have one but I've never read it," Mimsey said. "I tried once but couldn't understand it."

Abigail knew just what Mimsey needed. She went to the cabinet where she kept spare Bibles and took out a new one for her friend.

"Here is a copy of an NIV study Bible just for you," Abigail said. "It's my favorite version of the Bible, and it includes commentary to help you understand God's Word."

"Thank you so much, Abigail," Mimsey said as she took the Bible and began to flip through its pages. "I can't wait to start reading this. I am already feeling so much better.

"I know that God has forgiven me, but I think it's going to take a while before I can forgive myself," Mimsey said.

"Oh, Mims, it was so hard for me to forgive myself, but one night while I was driving I heard a life-changing message on the radio. The DJ was talking about how many Christians struggle with forgiving themselves. They act like they need more than Jesus' forgiveness to be able to forgive themselves. The DJ then asked the question 'What more do you want? What else can God possibly do for you? He sent His one and only Son to die on the cross. That's all you need.' That message opened my heart to see that God has done it all—he has paid the price for my sins. I had to accept that."

"Wow, I guess I never thought of it like that," Mimsey said.

"Watching you accept Jesus has been the highlight of my day—maybe even my year," Abigail said as she gave her friend a huge hug. "I feel so blessed that God allowed me to be a part of it."

"Thank you for sharing your love of Jesus with me," Mimsey said.

"Well now you've got it and you've taken the first step to your new life with Christ," Abigail said. "Pray that God will give you wisdom and direction for your journey. I will be praying for you and I'm always here for you anytime day or night. I may not always have the answers, but I know the One who does."

"I can't wait to tell Jim!" Mimsey said. She had so much excitement built up inside of her that Abigail thought she might burst like an overfilled balloon. Abigail prayed silently that Mimsey would always have such joy and zeal for the Lord.

"You share your story and don't be afraid," Abigail encouraged. "Live a life that is full of joy, peace, and love, and Jim will want what you have, no doubt. Thank you for stopping by and for having the courage to share your story. I love you, girl!"

As Mimsey left, it was apparent that the weight she had carried into the shop had been lifted. Abigail sat in silence, in awe of the Lord. She prayed:

"Lord, please be with this new child of Yours. Show her Your ways. Thank you for allowing me the opportunity to watch Mimsey come to know You. I am humbled that You would choose me. I love You, Lord. In Jesus' most precious name, Amen."

Trust in the Lord with all of your heart and lean not on your own understanding; in all your ways acknowledge him, and he will make your paths straight.

Proverbs 3:5–6 (NIV)

chapter ten

The next day, Ruthie, Abigail, and Mimsey met for lunch at the Darling Diner. They were greeted by the aroma of the daily special–chicken noodle soup and mashed potatoes served with a homemade roll.

The daily special was always served with a short devotion from *Chicken Soup for the Soul*. Guests' physical and spiritual appetites were always fed and they left satisfied.

The owners of the diner, Angie and Lisa, had transformed an old railroad caboose into a place where guests could not only experience a great home cooked meal, but also get a taste of Jesus' love. The caboose was deep red and trimmed in black. Black and white striped awnings hung over the windows. The interior of the caboose was just as enjoyable as the exterior. Clocks of many different shapes and sizes adorned the walls. The words "It's Time to Eat" were painted on the wall above the counter where guests sat to enjoy their meals.

Each day, Angie and Lisa prayed over the meals that they prepared. Customers knew they could ask for prayer; it said so on the menu. When Angie and Lisa took orders, they would ask their guests, "How can we pray for you?"

Angie and Lisa liked to think of the diner as a prayer diner. Whatever it was, God was using them to make a difference in the lives of others, even if it was one prayer at a time.

Ruthie loved Angie and Lisa because of their kindness and because every day they provided a hot meal for her, on the house. Ruthie didn't know who bought her meals, but she felt like she needed to pass on the good fortune. Each day she shared her meal with Mrs. White, an elderly woman who lived on the north side of town. She couldn't think of anything better than sharing a hot meal and deep conversation about God's Word with a good friend.

Ruthie couldn't believe Mimsey had given Mrs. White a box identical to the one she had found. There was no way she would be able to eat lunch today. She had been up all night; her mind was spinning in a thousand different directions. What if Mrs. White left the box next to the dumpster?

The three friends sat at Ruthie's favorite booth and each ordered the daily special. They chatted quietly; all of them wondered what part Mrs. White played in the mystery.

Abigail couldn't help but notice the joy on Mimsey's face. She was bubbling with excitement over her salvation.

"Mimsey, how did it go last night? Did you have time to visit with Jim?" Abigail asked.

"Well, when I went home, Jim was watching TV and I asked if we could talk," Mimsey said. "I'm sure he knew something serious was up, because I usually just blurt out whatever is on my mind. Anyway, I shared with him my decision to serve Christ and to live a life pleasing to Him.

"Then I came clean about my past," Mimsey continued. "He was so kind and compassionate. I couldn't believe it. He said he's been feeling like something is missing in his life. I'm praying that Jim will accept Christ so that we can begin to serve the Lord together."

"Mimsey I am so happy for you," Abigail said, with a bright smile on her face. "I'm sure God has a big smile on His face right now!"

"Kind of like the one on your face?" Mimsey laughed. "I think I've finally experienced the joy of the Lord."

As Abigail and Mimsey laughed, Ruthie sat confused.

"Did I miss something?" Ruthie asked, feeling left out of the celebration.

Mimsey filled Ruthie in on the life-changing decision she had made the night before.

"Oh Mimsey, I'm amazed at how awesome our God is," Ruthie said.

About that time, their food arrived. Normally they took the time to read the short inspirational story that came with each meal. Today they were all distracted by Mimsey's great news and thoughts of the box.

"Will you bless the food, Abi?" Ruthie asked.

"I would love to," Abigail said.

She prayed: "Dear Heavenly Father, we thank you for this meal and for the hands that prepared it. We thank you for the beautiful day you have blessed us with and the time we have together. We thank You for our new sister. We praise Your name. We ask You to bless this food to the nourishment of our bodies. In the Mighty Name of Jesus, Amen."

After they had prayed and began to eat, Mimsey took her inspirational story and shared it with the group.

"The following words were written on the tomb of an Anglican Bishop in the Crypts of Westminster Abbey," she said.

When I was young and free and my imagination had no limits, I dreamed of changing the world. As I grew older and wiser, I discovered the world would not change, so I shortened my sights somewhat and decided to change only my country.

But it, too, seemed impossible.

As I grew into my twilight years, in one last desperate attempt, I settled for changing only my family, those closest to me, but alas, they would have none of it.

And now as I lie on my deathbed, I suddenly realize: If I had only changed myself first, then by example I would have changed my family.

From their inspiration and encouragement, I would then have been able to better my country and maybe even changed the world.

"Oh that is profound," Abigail said. "Ruthie, do you want to read yours?"

"Mine is called 'The Hand,'" she said as she began to read.

A Thanksgiving Day editorial in the newspaper told of a school teacher who asked her class of first graders to draw a picture of something they were thankful for. She thought of how little these children from poor neighborhoods actually had to be thankful for. But she knew that most of them would draw pictures of turkeys or tables with food. The teacher was taken aback with the picture Douglas handed in...a simple child-like hand. But whose hand? The class was captivated by the abstract image. "I think it must be the hand of God that brings us food,' said one child."A farmer" said another, "because he grows the turkeys." Finally when the others were at work, the teacher bent over Douglas's desk and asked whose hand it was. "It's your hand, Teacher," he mumbled.

"She recalled that frequently at recess she had taken Douglas, a scrubby forlorn child, by the hand. She often did that with the children. But it meant so much to Douglas. Perhaps this was everyone's Thanksgiving, not for the material things given to us but for the chance, in whatever small way, to give to others.

"Wow I always get the tear jerker," Ruthie said as tears welled up in her eyes.

"Ok, it's my turn." Abigail was ready to read hers. "Mine is called 'Risking.'"

To laugh is to risk appearing the fool.

To weep is to risk appearing sentimental.

To reach out for another is to risk involvements.

To expose feelings is to risk exposing your true self.

To place your ideas, your dreams, before the crowd is to risk their loss.

To love is to risk not being loved in return.

To live is to risk dying.

To hope is to risk despair.

To try is to risk failure.

But risks must be taken because the greatest hazard in life is to risk nothing.

The person who risks nothing does nothing, has nothing, and is nothing.

She may avoid suffering and sorrow, but she simply cannot learn, feel, change, grow, love, live.

Chained by her own fears, she is a slave: She has forfeited freedom.

Only a person who risks is free!

"Wow, not only did we have great food, but we had three great stories today," Mimsey said. "What more could we have asked for?"

"You know what, girls? I've been thinking and we haven't actually asked God to show us the owner of the box," Abigail said. "Let's pray again and ask Him for wisdom and to guide our paths."

Abigail prayed: "Dear Lord, You are the maker of Heaven and Earth; You created each one of us. You know all things. So we come before You and ask that You would reveal to us the owner of the box. If it is Your will that we find this sweet person, we ask that You guide and direct our every step. We thank You in advance for introducing us to Evelyn. We praise Your name. In Jesus' name, Amen."

"Now what should we do?" Mimsey asked.

"I need to take this food to Mrs. White before it gets cold," Ruthie said. "Would you ladies like to go with me?"

Ruthie had never taken anyone with her during her visits with Mrs. White, but she knew that Mrs. White would love the company. Ruthie had told her so much about Abigail and Mimsey already.

The ladies paid for their lunch and piled into Abigail's car.

"Hey, Ruthie, do you think we could ask Mrs. White if she still has the box I gave her?" Mimsey asked. "Or do you think that's being too nosey?"

"We'll see how the conversation goes," Ruthie said. "If we can work the box into the conversation we will. Let's trust that God will open the door for us."

No eye has seen, no ear has heard, no mind has conceived what God has prepared for those who love him—but God has revealed it to us by His spirit. The Spirit searches all things, even the deep things of God.

1 Corinthians 2:9–10 (NIV)

chapter eleven

Abigail pulled her car up to a simple adobe house, not much bigger than the shed Ruthie lived in.

The ladies got out of the car and headed towards the door. They could see Mrs. White through the front window. It was obvious she had been waiting for Ruthie to arrive. Mrs. White appeared in the doorway. Abigail was surprised to see that she was in a wheelchair. She thought it was odd that neither Ruthie nor Mimsey had mentioned the chair. Mrs. White opened the screen door and greeted them.

"Come in, ladies, to what do I owe this visit?" Mrs. White asked. Abigail could tell she was surprised to see them, but also happy to have the company.

Mrs. White wore a plum-colored pantsuit made of silk, and her dark black hair was twisted into an elegant chignon. Her face was splattered with wrinkles that seemed to disappear when she smiled. She smelled sweet, like fresh-baked sugar cookies.

A table and chair obviously meant for Mrs. White and Ruthie greeted the women as they stepped into the quaint home.

Mrs. White apologized for the lack of seating and invited Mimsey and Abigail to grab two folding chairs that were tucked away behind the door. They unfolded the chairs and sat them around the table. As they sat down, Mrs. White wheeled her chair closer to the table.

Abigail noticed that Mrs. White kept her house very tidy and the aroma of cinnamon filled the air.

"Now that we're settled, why don't you introduce me to your friends," Mrs. White said as she patted Ruthie's hand.

Abigail was touched by the gesture. Something about the warmness in Mrs. White's voice made Abigail feel very comfortable, even though she had only just met the woman.

"Mrs. White, you know Mimsey, don't you?" Ruthie asked. "She's your land lady."

"I thought that was you," Mrs. White said as she squeezed Mimsey's hand. "At my age, sometimes it's easier just to ask to be introduced to someone than to risk calling them the wrong name. Forgive me for not recognizing you. I don't know how I could have forgotten you after you brought me that delicious meal in that gorgeous box."

Before Mimsey had a chance to ask Mrs. White whether or not she still had the box, she turned to face Abigail.

"I'm pretty sure we haven't met." Mrs. White said, smiling a radiant smile.

Ruthie began to introduce Abigail to Mrs. White, but before she could finish Mrs. White stopped her.

"Oh, yes. I should've known," she said. "You're Abigail. Ruthie has told me so much about you and the precious friendship the two of you share."

Abigail and Ruthie laughed. Abigail stood up, went over to Mrs. White and gave the woman a hug. When Mrs. White wrapped her arms around Abigail, she could feel the love of the Lord envelop her.

"It is so nice to finally meet you," Abigail said. "I feel like I already know you from all the wonderful things that Ruthie has told me."

Ruthie poured a glass of iced tea for Mrs. White and placed it in front of her, along with the chicken noodle soup. Mrs. White chatted with her company as she ate her lunch.

"Mimsey, tell me more about yourself," Mrs. White said. "I know you sell insurance and manage rental property, but what else should I know about you?"

Mimsey was so excited that Mrs. White wanted to know more about her. She couldn't wait to tell her all the wonderful things that had been going on in her life.

"I have known these girls for a while," Mimsey said as she pointed to Abigail and Ruthie. "But just last night I became their sister in Christ. I am so excited about my new relationship with Jesus I can barely contain myself. I'm reading my Bible and I'm going to start attending Bible study at Abigail's house."

"Oops! there I go again," Mimsey said. "I get pretty wound up talking about all that God has done in my life lately."

"Don't apologize, Mimsey. You can share how God is moving in your life with me anytime," Mrs. White said. "I love the enthusiasm of a new believer. It is music to my ears."

Mimsey decided there was really no reason to wait to ask Mrs. White about the box she had given her. Before she could stop herself she blurted out the question she had been dying to ask.

"Mrs. White, you mentioned the gorgeous box I delivered your meal in," Mimsey said. "Do you happen to still have that?"

"I'm sorry, Mimsey. I thought the box was so beautiful that I passed it on to someone else. Did you want it back?"

"Oh no, Mrs. White, I don't need it back," Mimsey said. "I was just curious if you still had it, because Ruthie found one exactly like yours next to one of the dumpsters here in town."

Ruthie and Abigail gave Mimsey a stern look. She could tell they weren't happy that she had spilled the beans.

"Mrs. White, we need to get going," Ruthie said. "Sorry we can't stay longer but Abigail needs to get back to her shop. I'll be by tomorrow with your lunch." Ruthie bent down to hug her friend.

"Girls, this has been such a delight, why don't you all come back for lunch tomorrow?" Mrs. White said. "I've enjoyed your company so much and would love to get to know you better."

As the four women hugged and said their goodbyes, Abigail and Mimsey agreed to join them again.

Mrs. White watched as the three women got into their car and drove away. The following day, she would reveal her connection to the box.

— —

Ruthie, Abigail, and Mimsey drove back to the shop in complete silence. Mimsey felt awful for opening her mouth about the box. She had never been good at keeping secrets.

When they were back at the shop, sitting around the dining table, Mimsey finally spoke.

"I'm really sorry," she said. "It's just that I felt so comfortable talking to Mrs. White. I was sure she could help if she had known anything about the box."

Ruthie patted Mimsey's hand. She wasn't mad at her friend. How could she be? She was only trying to help.

"You know, Mimsey, I'm thinking that Mrs. White might be able to help us solve this mystery," Ruthie said. "She seems to be a very wise woman. Maybe we should tell her the whole story when we have lunch with her tomorrow. Maybe she'll tell us who she gave the box to and that will lead us to the person who left it by the dumpster."

"Really?" Abigail and Mimsey said in unison.

"What could it hurt?" Ruthie said.

Peace I leave with you; my peace I give to you. I do not give to you as the world gives. Do not let your hearts be troubled and do not be afraid.

John 14:27 (NIV)

chapter twelve

After a quick stop at the Darling Diner to pick up Mrs. White's lunch, Ruthie, Abigail, and Mimsey arrived at the small adobe house to find Mrs. White waiting for them on the porch.

Her black hair was swept into a classic bun, and she wore a silk suit similar to the one she had worn the previous day. Today's suit of choice was a rich brown, the color of dark chocolate.

Ruthie noticed Mrs. White looking inquisitively at the green box under her arm. She could tell it must have been an exact replica of the one Mimsey had given her.

Mrs. White greeted each of the women with a smile and a hug before inviting them inside. Mimsey noticed that the folding chairs were already placed

around the table, as were four china teacups filled
with steaming hot tea.

Ruthie opened the carryout box from the
Darling Diner and placed it in front of Mrs. White.
The smell of pot roast and potatoes filled the air.

"Have you already eaten?" Mrs. White asked.

"Yes," Abigail said. "We grabbed a bite at the
diner before we came."

Ruthie noticed that Mrs. White kept glanc-
ing at the box, which she had slid under her chair.
Ruthie wanted to give her friend time to eat before
telling her the story.

Before Mrs. White had even taken a bite of her
pot roast she said, "Ladies, I have a confession to
make. I know about the box."

Stunned, the three friends leaned forward in
their seats. Just when they thought they were about
to surprise Mrs. White, she had surprised them.

"My name is Evelyn White," she continued.

Shock and disbelief filled the faces of her guests.

"You're Evelyn? You're the owner of the box?"
Ruthie exclaimed.

"Yes," Mrs. White said. "I'm afraid I probably
have a lot of explaining to do. I think you'll under-

stand the meaning behind the box after I share my story with you."

"We're finally going to find out the mystery behind the box," Mimsey exclaimed. "We have been racking our brains trying to figure out who Evelyn was and why she would have left a box full of so many valuable things in a pile of trash."

"Mims, let's give Mrs. White a chance to share her story," Abigail said. Ruthie nodded.

Mrs. White pushed the plate of untouched food aside.

"When I was seventeen years old, I met a man and fell head-over-heels in love. We were married as soon as I graduated from high school and were barely making ends meet. I managed a sandwich and ice cream shop and he drove a local delivery truck. To make extra money, we both decided to get second jobs working at night. We started working in a bar, but quickly realized that a bar wasn't the place for a married couple to be. It wasn't long before my husband had an affair. I was so hurt by his indiscretions that I decided to have an affair too. I thought it would feel good to pay him back for the pain he had caused me. After my affair, our marriage continued to spiral out of control and eventually ended in divorce.

"I had been raised in church, but when one of the members discovered my affair and the divorce, she told me the church would be a better place if I wasn't there.

"My life continued to get uglier, but I hid the pain from my friends and family. I drank and partied way too much. I was constantly searching for someone or something to fill the empty places in my heart, most of the time it was men. At the time, I worked with a woman who was married to a preacher. There was something very intriguing about her. She had a sweet spirit and joy exuded from the depths of her soul. One Sunday she invited me to go to church with her.

"I was hesitant to step foot in another church. All I could think about was being shunned from church after my divorce. I explained my hesitation to the woman, but she reassured me that I would be accepted with open arms at her church.

"That Sunday I gave my life to Jesus Christ. Although I still needed to make a lot of changes in my life, I had something that I had never had before, hope. Becoming a Christian didn't erase all the pain of my past, and some days were harder than others. Even though I had a relationship with Jesus, I still struggled with guilt. Many times I would buy into the lie the devil wanted me to believe, that I was a failure.

"Not long after I gave my life to Jesus, another man stepped into my life and promised to take care of me. After a short courtship, we were married. The funny thing is I never had peace about marrying him. I knew in my heart that the marriage wasn't what God wanted for me. But I did marry him, and shortly after the wedding, I discovered I was pregnant.

During the pregnancy, my husband began to drink a lot. He became very controlling. After I gave birth to our daughter, Michelle, I knew I couldn't stay with him. I was terrified that he would hurt one of us

"I had no idea how I was going to raise a baby on my own. I became hopeless and started thinking that it would be easier if I just killed myself.

"My daughter was only a month old when I started having suicidal thoughts. I knew of a family who desperately wanted a child. I knew they would take care of her and give her a home.

"I wrote a letter to the couple telling them they could have my child. I took all of her things and left them, along with the letter, on the couple's porch. I knew the precious lady that lived across the street and took Michelle to her. I asked her to watch the baby until the couple returned home.

"When I got home I took a whole bottle of pills. I woke up in the hospital two days later with bigger problems than I had started with. I was admitted to a state hospital, but I didn't care. I knew my daughter was safe and that's all that mattered to me. She went to live with the family I had hoped would adopt her and they eventually did.

"While I was in the hospital, I discovered my second husband was being indicted for past sexual crimes with children. I was repulsed at the thought of him. I was granted an emergency, medical divorce.

"I was still struggling with thoughts of suicide and enormous amounts of guilt. I was supposed to be a child of God wasn't I? How could I have done so many terrible things? I didn't know how I would ever be able to ask God to forgive me for the many sins I had committed. I had given up my child, tried to take my life, and had two failed marriages. I was certainly not living the way the Bible instructed me to.

"One day my pastor came to visit and he shared the story of his daughter's suicide with me. Hearing my pastor talk about his daughter, so much grief still apparent in his voice, made me realize I was very selfish for trying to take my life. I was God's child; suicide was not the answer to my problems.

"During his visit, my pastor handed me a small sheet of yellow paper. He encouraged me to read the words written on the note at least once a day. He said he didn't just want me to read it, but believe it. After he left, I unfolded the piece of paper and read the words he had written."

Mrs. White closed her eyes and from memory started to recite the words that had been inscribed on the note so many years ago.

"I am deeply loved, totally forgiven, fully pleasing, accepted and complete in Christ," she said.

"I remember seeing that note tucked into the pages of the Bible that was in the box," Ruthie interrupted.

"I have kept the note all these years," Mrs. White said. "Reading those words made me realize that God does not force us to do His will. He has a plan for our lives, but we can choose to go our own way."

"I think we have all tried to go our own way in life," Abigail said. "I know that I have."

Mimsey and Ruthie nodded their heads in agreement.

"It was while I was in the hospital that I discovered one of my favorite Bible verses," Mrs. White said. "I fell in love with Jeremiah 29:11 and decided I was tired of living outside of God's will for my life. I needed Him and wanted Him to show me the plan He had for me.

"I left the hospital a different person. I was committed to living my life for the Lord and seeking His will in all things. I had a group of women who encouraged me each day. Through their support and the richness of God's word, I was set free from the bondage of suicidal thoughts."

Abigail knew what it felt like to be set free from the bondage of sin. As Mrs. White continued to share her story, Abigail started to see the common threads that tied the four women together. They had all been through many difficult things in their lives, but they had all experienced the incredible grace of their savior.

Mrs. White continued.

"About three years after I was released from the hospital, I met a man named Jack. He was a pastor, recently divorced. I decided that if God could use a divorced man to further His kingdom, he could certainly find a way to use me, despite my rocky past.

"It wasn't long after I met Jack that he asked me to marry him. He wanted me to join him in ministry, sharing the love of God with the hurting people of the world. God was answering my prayer. He was using me, a sinful woman, to be His hands and feet in a hurting world."

"Jack and I were working in a women's shelter in Kansas. One day a woman named Chelle came in, her face badly bruised. Something about the woman grabbed my attention. She looked familiar, but her face was so swollen it was hard to place if I had ever met her before. The woman had a young son named James and it was obvious that he was really angry. Jack began to talk to the young boy while I got an ice pack for Chelle's face.

Ruthie wept silently as she listened to Mrs. White. Images of her daughter, Margaret, flashed through her mind. Abigail noticed and reached across the table and took Ruthie's hand.

"While Jack tended to James, Chelle shared with me that she was a prostitute," Mrs. White said. "She also had AIDS and a drug addiction. Her son had been in and out of foster homes since he was four."

"Chelle and her son stayed at the shelter for several months, and during that time Jack and I grew to love them. One day Chelle told me that she had never met her birth mother. She said her mother had left her with a couple when she was a month old and had tried to commit suicide.

"I couldn't contain my composure as Chelle shared her story with me. I was shaking violently and tears were flowing from my eyes. Before I could stop myself I had Chelle in my arms and was confessing that I was the woman who had left her so many years before.

"Michelle died a month later. I grieved the fact that I had lost my little girl for a second time and would never have the chance to get to know her. We had a memorial service for Chelle in the small prayer room at the shelter.

"James stayed with us for a while, but was eventually placed back into foster care. It broke our hearts to lose him, but social services wouldn't allow us to adopt him since I had abandoned his mother when she was a baby. He was eventually adopted by a family, but it wasn't long before they realized they couldn't deal with all the baggage of James's past. They sent him back to foster care, where he stayed until he maxed out of the system at the age of eighteen.

"James came to visit us once and we tried desperately to love him and make him feel accepted. It wasn't long after his visit that he got a job harvesting wheat fields here in town. One night while he was at a party, he met a sweet girl named Margaret. He was intrigued with her from the moment he met her. It wasn't long before he married her and they moved to Chicago. They said they were tired of the small-town life; they wanted to experience the excitement of a big city."

Ruthie was sobbing uncontrollably. Abigail couldn't believe what she was hearing.

"I don't understand," Mimsey said with a look of confusion on her face. "Ruthie, what's wrong?"

"Margaret was Ruthie's daughter," Abigail said. "She was married to James. He murdered Margaret and then killed himself."

Evelyn and Ruthie's hands were clasped tightly together. They were no longer just sister's in Christ; they were bonded together by grief. Tears streamed down Mimsey's face. She couldn't believe the tragedy; the pain in their eyes.

"After the murder/suicide, Jack and I decided to retire," Mrs. White said. "The tragedy of losing my only grandchild and his precious wife was more than my heart could bear. We decided to move here. We thought a quiet, small town would be just what we needed to grieve our loss."

"We fell in love with a beautiful house that had a wrap-around porch and hardwood floors. There was a garage for Jack to tinker in and a yard big enough for me to plant a garden. We both dreamed of living in that house, but it was way out of our price range.

"Shortly after we moved, Jack's aunt passed away. On our way to her funeral, I fell asleep in the car and had a dream that the house with the wrap-around porch would one day become a women's retreat center. I dreamt it would be a safe place for women, a place where they would be safe from harm and could learn about Jesus."

Once again, Abigail couldn't believe what she was hearing. Mrs. White had dreamt of opening a women's retreat center just like she had. She got the weird sensation of looking at her future self.

Mrs. White continued, "I was jolted awake in the middle of my dream to the sound of scraping metal and squealing tires. I heard what sounded like a million windows shattering.

"When I finally realized what was happening, I saw that our car had been hit by a truck carrying plate glass. In the seat next to me was my husband's lifeless body. Shards of glass filled the car, and I was bleeding from numerous cuts all over my body. I wanted to scream, but for some reason I couldn't. I tried to move but my body hurt so badly that it was like I was frozen. I would later discover that I was paralyzed. The last thing I remember was slowly losing consciousness.

"I woke up in the hospital a widow, unable to walk. All I could think about was Exodus 15:26. I repeated the words over and over in my mind and many times spoke the words out loud. 'I am the LORD, Your healer.'

"Time passed and the Lord healed me emotionally, but I never walked again. I'm not sure why God didn't physically heal me, but I knew that my wheelchair would not get in the way of His plan. His word promised that He would complete the good work that He had started in me.

"I knew I was supposed to come back here once I got out of the rehab hospital, but I had no idea how I would take care of myself. Several days before I was released from the hospital, I got a phone call from Jack's cousin. After her mother passed away, she found a gift that had been intended for Jack and me. Jack's aunt never had the chance to mail it before she died. Jack's niece said she would send the gift to me because she knew her mother would have wanted me to have it. A few days later I received a card from Jack's cousin. Inside was a letter written by his aunt."

Mrs. White pulled an envelope out of her pocket. She removed the faded letter and began to read.

> Dearest Jack and Evelyn,
>
> I have been praying for you now that you have retired. I would like you to use this gift to further your ministry. I know you have retired, but I sense that God still has many things to accomplish through you.
>
> > Love
> >
> > Aunt Ruby

"What was the gift?" Mimsey exclaimed. The tears that had once filled the room had been replaced with excitement.

"Inside the card was a check for $400,000," Mrs. White said. "I nearly fainted when I saw all those zeros. I knew immediately what God wanted me to do with the gift. He wanted me to buy the house that Jack and I had fallen in love with and open up the women's retreat center I had dreamed about.

"I bought the house as soon as I got out of the hospital, with money to spare. I intended to open the center quickly, but my injury kept me from fulfilling my plan." Mrs. White said. "I didn't know that God would be sending some special people into my life who would be able to help me fulfill the dream."

"So, how does the box fit in?" Ruthie asked.

"Ruthie, I had seen you roaming the alleys many times and something about you intrigued me," Mrs. White said. "The Lord placed it upon my heart that you were going to be the one who helped me fulfill my dream. I decided I would pay for your gas and meals with some of the money that was left over from Aunt Ruby's gift. I never dreamed you would eventually start sharing those meals with me and we would become such dear friends."

Ruthie hugged Mrs. White. She couldn't believe how intertwined their lives were.

"You don't know what a blessing your gift has been to me," Ruthie said. "Not just the free gas and meals, but the gift of your friendship."

"During one of our conversations, you mentioned your daughter Margaret, and that's when I realized that we were connected by a terrible tragedy," Mrs. White said. "I think that's when God affirmed to me that you were definitely supposed to be a part of the women's ministry I wanted to start.

"As I prayed about opening a retreat center, all I could think about was Margaret. She had a heart for women and children and wanted them to be cared for and loved. When I learned she had lost her life at the hand of her abuser, my grandson, I promised God that I would somehow continue the amazing work that she had started."

"It wasn't long before Ruthie began to tell me about Abigail and how she, too, dreamed of helping women and children in need. After several conversations about Abigail, I was certain that God wanted me to give the house to the two of you."

Abigail and Ruthie looked at each other shocked and speechless, while Mimsey squealed with delight.

"I knew that if I offered the box to Ruthie, she wouldn't have taken it. That's why I asked Angie, from the diner, to place the box by the dumpster. I knew that Ruthie would find it and take it to you, Abigail. I knew that you would search through the books, connect all the dots, and discover that I was the owner," Mrs. White said. "My wish and what I believe is God's plan, is for the two of you to open a retreat center for women. The money inside the box will be enough to get your ministry started."

Abigail and Ruthie were still speechless but humbled by Mrs. White's generosity and confidence in them. They couldn't believe they had the resources they needed to start a ministry like they had dreamed of doing. They would finally be able to help other women who had traveled the same familiar roads they had been down.

"I think Ruthie found the box at the exact time she was supposed to," Abigail said. "God has definitely used this adventure to strengthen the bond between the three of us."

"That's true," Ruthie said. "If Abigail hadn't shared her story with me after seeing the Bible, I don't think I would have ever shared my story with her. Because of the box, we have bonded in ways we probably never would have."

"I agree," Mimsey said. "It seems like God always has a way of bringing people into your life at just the moment you need them. This time he just happened to use a box full of wonderful treasures to fulfill His plan."

"Mrs. White, what about the other things in the box?" Ruthie asked. "I know you said the Bible belonged to you, but I'm curious about the bag of pearls. What's the story behind them?"

Oh, the story behind the pearls is a beautiful one indeed," Mrs. White said. "Are you sure you have time to stick around to hear it?"

"Mrs. White, if you think I could go home after all the excitement we've had here today, you're crazy," Mimsey teased.

"Before I get to the story behind the pearls, I think it's important that you know why I included the books," Mrs. White said. "The books that I included in the box were some of my favorite ones from the shelter. I had purchased them and loaned them to many women, hoping they would experience Jesus' touch. The names written inside each book belong to all the women who borrowed the books. Each one of the women got to hear about God's great love for her."

"Wow, that's an amazing way to witness to others," Ruthie said. "There were so many names written in all of those books."

"Enough about the books," Mimsey said impatiently. "Where did you get all of those pearls?"

Mrs. White chuckled.

"The pearls in the box were a gift from my mother," Mrs. White said as she reached up to touch a strand that hung around her neck. "The pearls that I'm wearing were a gift from Jack. I love pearls because they remind me of the sacrifice that Jesus made for my sin. They are a symbol of purity, of something beautiful. Christ died for my ugly and dirty sins, and in return gave me the beautiful gift of eternal life."

Mimsey cleared her throat and tears filled her eyes.

"Mrs. White, I know that you put the box by the dumpster for Ruthie and Abigail to find, but I want you to know that it had a huge impact on me. Because of that box, I received Christ," Mimsey said choking back tears. "For that, I will be forever grateful."

Abigail watched as Ruthie took Mimsey's hand and gave it a squeeze.

"So," Mimsey asked, looking at Ruthie and Abigail. "What are you going to call the retreat center?"

Abigail looked at Ruthie and then at Mrs. White.

"The Peace House," she said. "I pray it's a place where women will experience God's peace and His amazing love."

The four women raised their tea cups and made a toast to their amazing God and to the journey they were about to embark on.

books and music
that inspire

- *The Holy Bible*–This is my favorite book…

- *Breaking Free* by Beth Moore–I received an incredible amount of healing through this book. I was set free from the bondage of my past sins and shame when I laid them all at the feet of Jesus. I hope anyone who has ever made bad choices, as I have, will take the opportunity to go through this amazing study. The study will guide you as you ask for and receive forgiveness and you will be restored by the incredible, amazing love of Jesus.

- *The Greatest Miracle in the World* by Og Mandino–Through this book, I discovered what a ragpicker was, and desired to become one. I also learned that God has given every person the power to think, the power to love, the power to will, the power to laugh, the power to imagine, the power to create, the power to plan, the power to speak, and the power to pray. We are His ultimate creation, and His greatest miracle. I also learned to wisely use my power of choice. Choose to love rather than hate. Choose to laugh rather than cry. Choose to create rather than destroy. Choose to persevere rather than quit. Choose to praise rather than gossip. Choose to heal rather than wound. Choose to give rather than steal. Choose to act rather than procrastinate. Choose to grow rather than rot. Choose to pray rather than curse. Choose to live rather than die.

- *The Practice of the Presence of God with Spiritual Maxims* by Brother Lawrence–Through this book, I learned what it meant to be in God's presence at all times. I became more aware of God's presence even when I was doing mundane tasks, such as washing the dishes.

- *Running the Red Lights* by Charles Mylander - This book really reiterated to me that Christ loved me, no matter what I had done. In fact, He delights in forgiving the worst of sexual sin and rebuilding the lives of those who suffer its consequences. The Bible gives us plenty of examples: For David it was adultery, for Samson it was compulsive lust, for Gomer it was a series of illicit affairs, for some of the Corinthians, it was homosexual sin, and with an unnamed church member in Corinth, it was incest. Jesus didn't say to these people, "clean up your act and then come to me." He simply said, "Come."

- *The Long Love Letter* by Margaret Ruth Baker– Through this book, I fell in love with God's Word and it became even more alive and personal to me. Margaret has amplified God's Word into a Long Love Letter addressed to me and you. I hope and pray that you will read this book and experience God's Word in a way that you never have before.

- *Same Kind of Different as Me* by Denver Moore and Ron Hall - This book is based on a true story.

After reading it, I was encouraged to ask God exactly what His plan and purpose was for my life. God can use anyone, no matter what their past looks like. Through this book, God gave me the desire to reach out beyond myself and make a positive difference in the lives of others.

• *Crazy Love* by Francis Chan—As a result of this book, I want the love I have for Jesus to overflow onto those around me. I was also reminded that if I stop pursuing Christ, I am letting our relationship deteriorate. Francis Chan also helped me to see that our view of the Holy Spirit is too small. The Holy Spirit who lives inside of us, is the One who changes the church, who changes us. It is individual people living Spirit-filled lives, who will change the church.

The Music That Has Touched My Heart

"Pure" by Kari Jobe

"Revelation Song" by Kari Jobe

"Amazing Grace My Chains are Gone"
by Chris Tomlin

"Touch Me Lord" by the Parachute Band

"Just Give Me Jesus" by Fernando Ortega

"Amazing Love, You are My King" by Hillsong

"I Exalt You" by Jesus Culture

"Holy, Holy, Holy! Lord God Almighty!" A Hymn